Specimen Sight-Reading Tests for Trombone 𝄞 and 𝄢

Grades 1–5

ABRSM

Printed in England by Caligraving Ltd, Thetford, Norfolk,
on materials from sustainable sources
Reprinted in 2018

GRADE 1

AB 2485

GRADE 1

AB 2485

GRADE 2

GRADE 2

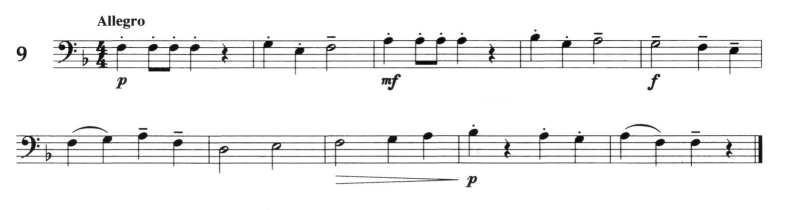

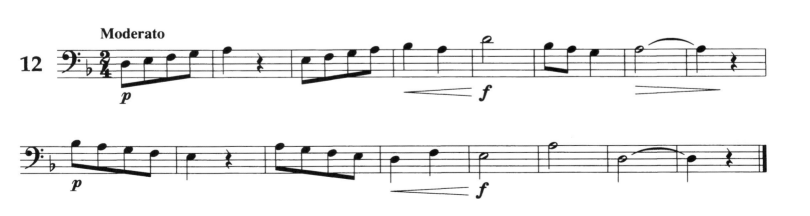

GRADE 3

AB 2485

GRADE 4

AB 2485

GRADE 4

Risoluto

5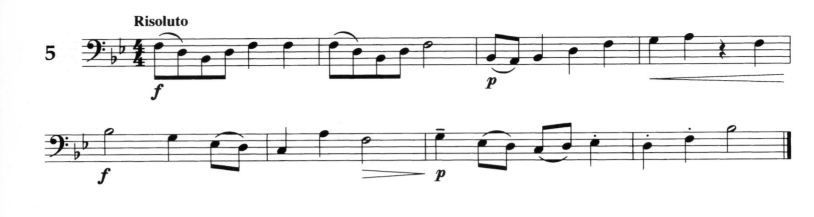

Allegro

6

Grazioso

7

Moderato

8

GRADE 5